Power
of
Words

Molly Thokwana

Pharos Books

ISBN: 978-93-91384-07-4
eISBN: 978-93-91384-13-5

©Publishers

Publisher: Pharos Books (P) Ltd.
Plot No.-55, Main Mother Dairy Road
Pandav Nagar, East Delhi-110092
Phone: +14049995474, +91 011-40395855
WhatsApp: +14049995474
E-mail: sales@pharosbooks.in
Website: www.pharosbooks.in
Edition: 2021
Printed By: Sushma Book Binding House, Okhla
Industrial Area, Phase II, New Delhi-110020

Power of Words
Author: *Molly Thokwana*

INTRODUCTION

Power of Words is a motivational book that describes that purpose on its own is an inspiration. For you to read this book you needed inspiration and reason, of which I gave reason and understanding of why I wrote this book.

In life, we all need a purpose to do something and make something out of it. The reality is between objecting to creating something and how to create it.

We are trapped between having the knowledge and having insight into what we want to do. We always need a purpose to inspire us to do something, yet our own worth can't even inspire us to do something.

All we need is to believe in ourselves, that with or without a purpose our self-worth inspires us.

This book holds challenges that we go through in times of success and failure, how to choose to overcome them and the real principles of how we deal with such things. As people, we need to know how to have balance in the things we do. They say leaders should lead by example, but I say a leader who's willing to lead should be willing to overcome with followers.

PREFACE

I have realized that a lot of people are lost due to a lack of reasons for their faith and hope. They taught me that hope is to walk in the unseen and to long for what cannot be seen. I considered that since a lot of people seemed to be lost and they had hope and faith but with no reasons to why they hope and why they have faith.

Faith is the act of the unseen. If you can provoke your hope with what you can't see, then how hard can it be to anticipate for what you know. So, I discovered that we needed the drive to understand what really it is, that we want so that we can make a plan of what to do next.

Coming to the conclusion of all this I came to words that our power is vested in words and for us to do something we need to use words and without words, we can't use faith, hope, or even have a purpose. So, I birthed a small purpose and called it *Power of Words*.

A silence written in words but heard. This is not just the book you thought you could read, it's the book you never read that will change your life. It's not only going to change your life and change your thoughts, but it will give you a purpose through words.

This book has been my greatest challenge, to define what I can overcome and what we need to purpose in our hearts to know how to overcome it. It's all about knowing how to come out of that situation and how to control your time and how to take over when your season arrives.

ACKNOWLEDGEMENTS

With my first most appreciation, I thank God for the wisdom He has given me to write this book. Without your purpose and hope, I wouldn't have had the direction to know that I could complete and write like this.

I thank the grace I serve under Prophet Shepherd Bushiri, Prophetess Mary Bushiri, Prophetic Pastor Phitshane and Wiselady Bethel Phitshane. I thank God for such an encouraging rage that has helped me rise in life. Without your grace I would not have found it fit, to know and to acknowledge such an amazing presence in my life. I also thank Pastor Mbakhwa and his wife Segojame Mbakhwa for their prayers and their support.

For this book to have had been published, I am grateful to everyone who contributed to the publication of this book, and I thank my family, especially my mother, Judith Shatho Thokwana, for her unconditional support for everything I have done, though she is no more and I am also thankful to my brother Coffie Thokwana.

May God bless you and advance you for buying this book.

DEAR READER

You might probably be thinking "I have read so many books, what's so special about this one?" It's not about how special this book is; it is about what the book can do for you. I am heartedly grateful for your purchase of this copy. This book is your life transformation, the moment you bought it your life began to change. Even when I read it to the best of my ability, I still find myself being inspired by this book.

I bring you my purpose, written in a book and defined in a sense that is not found fit, but it's seen to be fit. When you read this book, may favor locate you. I have released this book to help and heal the broken and make the weak to be strong. Sometimes you have to hold on, even when it doesn't make sense because no trial is permanent. Everything passes in due time.

This book has made me realize that we should learn to practice what we speak. You achieve greater heights by working hard for them rather than boasting of them. The reason why I say this is my purpose is because I find worth in the power of words and what they can do to us and the power they hold. A journey is a path that destines how you started. You cannot face reality unless you do something to overcome it. You cannot buy a book if you don't believe that it can truly change your life.

We become weak to learn to be strong. We lose in life so we can see and get to know what we have beyond our capabilities. Our deepest capabilities are not found in what we have achieved, but in how far we can go. With every little trial we go through, it should help you understand how far you can go.

ABOUT THE AUTHOR

Molly Thokwana is a writer from Africa, Botswana, born on the 4th of July. She is the author of twenty-one published books and she's working on more upcoming books. She focuses on writing genres of short stories, motivational, adventurous, Christian writing, poetry, and articles. She has also been published in places such as South Africa, India, Hong Kong, France, and Botswana.

She is a graduate from Abm University College and holds an advanced diploma in Business Skills and holds other qualifications in the fields of accounting and archives and records the literature field.

She has completed her education from Aerodrome primary, Selepa junior, Mater-Spei College, Business technical college and furthermore progressed to Abm University College. She also shares some of her writings at poetmollymolz.wordpress.com.

She is also a creative writer along with a vocalist, songwriter with her music playing on online music channels. She has worked with various producers and her music can be found online as Poet Molz and her writing personality career as Molly Thokwana on google.

Contents

POWER OF WORDS

We hold so much power to change the way we interact with things around us. Our words give us the power to consider truth and change the way we look at some things. Words are powerful, as they take an act of what you send them to or what you want them to be.

Our power of words is associated with our character, our mind and our surrounding. There's a way that you interact with different people in different ways and different words. How you respond matters the most. Some people may see that what is wrong as right and what is right as wrong. It's very important to have wisdom and understand that how we relate and come to understand each other differ a lot. There is a precise power that determines how you see and perform things based on how you act and deal with situations and do things.

A man lived near the mountains where he got firewood; since he collected firewood annually he decided he should sell firewood in the city to earn money. He was willing to sell firewood, but he was not willing to invest in the business to earn more income. Words are also a commitment; you can commit to wanting to do something but without doing what you have committed it doesn't work well.

The question is, are we all willing to invest in everything that we do so we could earn more of what we have. We can commit to things with words and not act on them. Words have the power to change a lot of things, but a lot of people are used to saying anything they want at any time. The difference is what character does your way of explaining something and doing something have.

At what level are you willing to hold the power of words in you and make a change? We change if we only accept to take charge of what we want. The bible says, "Faith without works is dead". It is easy to admit what we can't do. So many people have a syndrome of, "I believe and I have faith". Then what's next? Your act can imply a thousand ways to your own change.

Our relationship with man is not distinguished by probabilities; it is strengthened by interactions and words. A fond relationship can be broken by just words. Many of our life choices were made by words and some of which ended up making life a misery for most of us.

You have been given the power that is your own freedom. Your ability to change doesn't come from speaking but also acting. The act to change and the act to be something happens when you have decided to change within you.

Don't undermine the power that your words have. For instance, today is probably one of those days where everyone feels success is probably what we possess or feel, and not what we do for the long term. Every word you start with determines your day all through. Success is not shown by the best suit, but by how long you can maintain that best suit. That's the problem with us we want to look at the part and forget we have to maintain the part.

Most people normally like to think that talking is nothing. But they lack the understanding that words can build us and also destroy us at the same time. Words hold the power that brings changes that can either be negative or positive. So, we must pay caution to what we say, when we say it and whom we say it to. Words can become a source and sense of comfort. Words are considered very expensive; they cost you your expression and timing and even your destiny. When your words are right, your timing becomes perfect. Words on their own bring change.

The power that words have can, at the end of the day, overpower us. Always make sure that the words you use are positive feedback or

 Power of Words

positive replies. Our positivity comes from how we view, interact and act upon things.

Your words can also be a reflection of your own life and how you live. In many instances, words have contributed to the loss of employment, friendships, and even concentration for some people. We can't know who we are or how to act until we have our own unique identity. We can lose direction because of wrong words.

Our words have the power to change how we think and can change our perspective and the way we do things. Words can't change our destiny, but they can transform how we look or face our destiny. We can't normally avoid words because they are our source of communication. The alternative of having powerful words works as a system. You can't fail your own understanding; you have to comprehend how you operate so that you can know how to control what you say.

We all have an effect that generates or demolishes what we are supposed to do and not what we were not supposed to do. There are stages that compete with the human mind. This basically defines when you have a diverse conversation with a person and automatically it tells you that there is truth in what is being said.

Every word that we hear communicates with us as truth. But some words send us a generated way of believing whether they are true or not true. It's how the human mind is. Like when we speak to someone our preliminary assumption is that the person is being honest. There should be an evident wave that tells us that the person is telling the truth.

The bible describes that Jesus spoke to the wind and rebuked the waves and said, "Peace be still". The symbolism of Jesus calming the storm should also give you the revelation of how powerful words can be. In the midst of your storms, you can calm them. **Mark 4 : 39**

COMING OUT

We all have those moments where we want to come out of our situations and be free. Being caged is not a good thing. You may have been feeling trapped for a long time, like nothing is really changing or nothing is moving in your life.

You try something out and it fails, or you move on with something and the past keeps coming back.

Nobody said the past won't haunt you, or that it won't be hard or that you won't fail to gain strength. I have been through hell to know heaven and I am sure that what I went through was a testimony, hence I could write this book to you and make you aware that if I came out then you will also come out.

Your grieving over your failures won't make you come out of that situation and you won't get out of it by sitting at home and hoping. You have to stand up and do something. Your problems might be minor than someone else's problems out there.

Imagine the grief that other people are facing, and you are there thinking your problems are too big. Nothing can be too big for God not to handle. God never gives us what we can't handle.

Moses was sent to free the Israelites to the promised land, and on the way, he was faced with a situation of the red sea, they couldn't cross over. Instead of giving up and not continuing with the journey, he believed in a way out with God. The red sea parted and he walked through that situation.

When you go through situations that's the time when your faith should grow so that you can defeat that situation. Our weaknesses should give us strength, not fail us. **Ephesians 2 : 8** says it is by grace we have been saved, by faith.

We don't go by our own timing but God's timing. Your time is just a mere thought that gives you hope. Imagine if we all had our own little timing where when we feel like doing something, we do it because we feel it's our time.

Nobody can predict the times of your season unless if God said so. We are moved by the word, to have the power to manifest within us.

We are caged because we all want a breakthrough but don't want to learn how to perceive one. Your weaknesses take you to your destination. I always hear people say "my greatest moment in life was when I was" which means they lived the moment to get to the moment. You have to be the moment to share all the moments.

Come out with the mentality that you can't make it, the people who thought they couldn't make it made sure that they made it. There is no one who can't admit that they haven't failed for them to achieve. Every beginning has its own challenges. Every success has its challenges written and kept. Every greatness has a testimony.

I have seen so many people who wanted to change and they ended up falling back to where they were because they were not ready to change but they were ready to show that they could change.

You cannot come out if you can't admit that you can face challenges. Change is not something that you purpose, but something you apply that you will work on it. It's a process.

Instead of applying change, we tend to create it for people to see it. We have all gone through challenges and we have all gone through the process of figuring out how to come out of all of them.

I had to come out of my situation; I am a walking testimony that went through fire to know how to set fire myself. I have been a victim and both a victor of how powerful words are and how powerful they can become. I don't know, maybe my perfect beginnings never taught me that life on its own has ups and downs, so I took the easy way that got me to the wrong side.

I don't really believe in small beginnings but the smaller I started, the bigger I became.

Here goes my story....

I grew up helping my mother with her business from an early age. I knew how profits would make me survive. My mother owned a mobile selling tuck-shop where she sold sweets, airtime, had a payphone and some assorted stuff. So, since I had finished my form three, I helped her while I was waiting for my exam results. She sometimes spent most of her time at work, so it was a work offload for her. Every time I felt fear tangle all sides of my body when I sat there selling.

I had fear, and it was bad because it haunted me many times and I hoped to overcome it. I couldn't speak and sometimes we lost customers because I could just say we don't have something while it was there because of fear. Business wasn't really that bad, but because I couldn't speak, it spoke less of me and I could have done a bit better. At times I hoped to be sick so that I wouldn't go sell and at times it couldn't be faked for too long. It was all we had in order to bring food to the table as it wasn't enough from what my mother got from work. My silence made a loss in so many ways that I could have changed my situations.

Even at school, I had a lot to say and sometimes when at home, I would rephrase what I could have said. To my conclusion, it's what I could have said that could have made me come out of my situation. Your words can change your life in a thousand ways.

The fact that we grow into habits and we think we can't make it, is the reason that makes us believe that we can't make it. Sometimes you have to stand out and come out, it's not about what you have been through but what you will be in the future. I came to notice that sometimes we want to come out, but we don't put effort to come out. No matter how hard it may look there will always be a way out.

I never knew, in the midst of my silence and fears of all those years, I would finally speak. I have found myself speaking powerful words to the youth and also giving guidance to many people. I found myself writing powerful words that impacted many people in a thousand ways. Because I came out and told myself it's time that I put everything aside and come out.

The thing is when you come out, learn to maintain it so it does not take you back. That's why we have so many Christians who backslide because after they come out of problems, they don't maintain their freedom.

NOT A VICTIM

No one said if you used to be a victim you should confess that you are one. Used to be its past tense, which means we speak the past that can't be reversed. I used to be a victim of words. I found it sincere to speak instead of putting my thoughts and implying exactly what my words meant.

I had a problem with time, and I had a challenge in keeping time. No matter where I was going or how far I was, I would lie that I was ten minutes nearer or five minutes away.

But don't we all sometimes put up with lies, aren't we all a victim of words at times? A little lie can turn into a bigger lie. No such thing as small habits, is there? If I had to describe and explain a bit further, I did say a lie is a word I used to cover myself up with when late. Beyond every lie, I believe there's a truth that created it. During my senior school days, I never went early to school. I always got there late, and I would get beaten at the gate so badly. Well, I hated time; I hated how time rules everything and how I can't rewind it back.

When I was young I believed in time machines, so every wrong I did, I pretended I went back in time and fixed it.

You see that's the beautiful part about being a kid, the way you think doesn't make sense sometimes and reality is just for the older people.

The more I grew and I got to understand that time was a problem. You see the thing was some habits we grow up with them and we fail to understand that they can affect us as time goes on. I felt it was just normal that I couldn't keep up with time. I felt people could understand my problem and relate, but they couldn't because my habit is not another person's habit. You see I knew I had a weakness, but I didn't think it could affect me that much in a way that I would lose job interviews as a graduate and stay home. To me if time was a person, I'd say, time is a cruel human being. A weakness that I grew up with thinking it was normal to have turned my life upside down.

A day, before Wednesday that is, I, the time skipper was called for an interview on a Friday. As a graduate I felt like it was the most remarkable moment of my life, to have gone this far to find a job in such a short time.

I have always wanted to work, but because I didn't have an option but to work or be homeless, I thought that getting a job would be the best thing I could have done. On a Thursday night, I had my best outfits ironed and hanged out. I was so excited; the life that I had always imagined was slowly getting closer. Money was mostly my primary inspiration in looking for a job, but you know life will humble you sometimes. You will answer even a phone call and say "yes job" instead of a hello.

I neatly took out my best shoes and I felt it, the excitement hit me so hard I imagined a shopping list before everything else. Friday came and the weather was so pleasant.

I woke up at 11 a.m. with a news broadcast that day and I could not believe this. All because of time, just time. My interview was supposed to have had been at 7 a.m. and imagine, the hours I spent sleeping.

A month passed, another interview, same old story? missing time and interviews. Here I am, feeling miserable with New Year's resolutions to five missed interviews just because I couldn't keep up with time. I woke up today at 6 a.m. to write this story to tell somebody. Never take habits lightly or think of them as small. A habit is a habit no matter how big or small it is you have to deal with it sooner. You are not a victim, but you have to change. Those of us who are victims it doesn't mean we should live forever as victims, it shall pass.

I have changed at this moment, and this change didn't come by saying I'm going to change. It came by me acting upon it. There are chapters below that are motivational in this book that will inspire someone to change. If time was my inspiration to change, then your self-worth should also be able to inspire you to change.

RESURRECT YOUR LIFE

Some people are dead yet alive, nothing moves in their lives. We are convinced that work monuments are a part of us, and they can be conquered and made free souls. We must resurrect the truth that prolongs some part in us that doesn't limit us from who we are or what we want to become.

It's like praying and receiving after you pray, yet you can pray and receive. You have to have that radical intervention that will change you in a minute and show you wonders in a minute. The problem with us is that we receive late, we decide late, we change late and want to overcome late. What if we lived in a world where tomorrow is now and so the emphasis between the two conjures a breakthrough. The power of words has a bigger possibility and positivity within us; we decide what we can do and how we can do it. Remember a student learns well by attending lessons, so resurrect yourself from assumptions and work to gain.

In some cases, challenges are the gateway to greatness, but a challenge that doesn't strengthen you came to fail your mind. Failure is what you accommodate and accompany in your life, when you decide to fail and give up that's when you accommodate failure.

Your life is not based in the hands of another, but you. Willingly you should have a moment where you separate the triangle facts of not tolerating circles that don't build up your life.

CONFRONTING THE INNER YOU

The inner you is not described by the outer you. There is war between the person you are on the outside and the inside. The difference is a character; it holds the deepest path to distinguish between the two.

Many of us have lost hopes in life that we believe only money fills, and we strain to get money also. The greatest amendments in life were done by people who believed in themselves. Confronting the inner you is never easy. It's letting go and moving on from who you were to who you will be. To overcome this some may need positive words they can wake up to every day as in:

1. Never pace when it comes to success, make your pace the patience of succeeding.

2. Hard work pays, but don't forget it pays when you work for it.

3. Second choices are there to make you better, make them make you greater.

4. Never let pain hurt you, make pain your motivation to inspire you to succeed.

5. Life gets better by choices of change not by chances.

6. Hardships are meant to strengthen us.

7. A royal is loyal by words not by thoughts.

The perspective of coming out of bondage is change and confronting the inner you. You are the one who can change who you are, but there's a different sense of attitude and character that one portrays in different ways which have to be dealt with.

Every person has a character in them, some people are not defined by works but by their characters. They are known by good and bad characters. The line between good and bad character is failure and gain. Your character can be your connection or your disconnection.

THE WORD

When you become the word, you and the word become one. The proper impact is to think before you speak and evaluate your decisions. Rest assured, the aim is not to act as a word but to be the word.

You are undertaken through a process of personnel's and dealing with characters, poor characters and those who think the world revolves around them, save a bit of what they can't withhold. An emphasis that describes the difference between change and changed shows that the two, fall under a process of going through something to get somewhere. The question is, are you powered enough to take the lead and make the word heard. The word is your voice, the silence that you have kept for so long while people stumbled and walked all over you. The word is the hate that was thrown to you with stones, anger and disappointment and you kept saying you will change, yet you didn't change. The word is the silence that is waiting for you to change something.

The word is saying it's fine when it is not all okay or has never been okay. For how long will it be just okay when it's not? Without words we have no goals to write, we have no focus. We live in scatter; the part of us has to be presented by something to be something. A direction that locates us, gives us reason to say something using words.

FAIL TO PASS

Whatever situation you may be going through today, remember other people have bigger problems than you do. There's no dream without a plan, we tend to make our decisions towards what we call a dead end.

Possibly because you do something because someone else is doing it and you think you can also do it. Anyone can do business but not all people have a business mind which can make them sustain a business.

I always tell people, the moment you decided to give up is the moment you failed. Failure doesn't come every day, there's an achievement in trying more to achieve something out of failure. Some people consider being subtle a heart-breaking moment that doesn't even make sense at times.

Some people do not care about inventors sometimes, some products sell without knowing who created them just by their names. But what they sometimes care most about is why should yours be considered rather than the other who is doing the same thing as you? Competition on its own at the level of the same products and passing to fail.

The idea is to have the need to be unique and to differ. No one can have the same taste elsewhere if they found it cheaper, but somebody can be willing to buy the product of the same name elsewhere if it tastes better and has better quality no matter how much the product is. Have a sense of loyalty and discipline. Create something to differ and pass.

Some people have no goals they just move around with the whole and to see what the day withholds for them. They try everything at any time because they don't know what they want. Some of you run away from trials because in the first place you were never ready for them.

There was no proper planning in what you are doing. You cannot want to pass if you can't handle failing. Your failures come as your biggest strength to a new level. Your failure was never a downgrade but it was your elevation. Your walks don't come paved, you have to pave your own way to get to another level.

STOP WORRYING

We spend so much time being worried about when the people we have helped will ever help us back. The truth is simply before us, not everyone is like you. We expect too much, we want too much, and we complain too much, yet we miss even our chances of doing something progressive with our lives.

There's always a reward in giving that can come in the form of knowledge, opportunities, help, and breakthrough. We are the ultimate reflection of our own kind.

Remember that what you lack or have, another person may have and lack. You seek help because it shows you are in need. Give help to show you have the need to help others.

I always quote that "poverty is what we accommodate". The less we think about ourselves is how even other people will view us. If you say you are sick and other people also see you are sick, it's how it portrays and what you accommodated. Poverty does not mean don't be smart or live a low life. You can still be poor but look rich. It's the stability in your mind that balances things, it shows you are going through a situation, but it doesn't mean that you agree with it.

Some people have the mentality of always worrying and complaining about things, if you see something that isn't right or doesn't suit your eyes, try to fix it. In my generation, I have met more complainers than achievers.

Young people these days are more concerned about having the right look to be rich instead of working hard to be rich. Our minds have failed us to have fun, rather achieve to invent fun. Life is what you make out of it and not in it, you invest to come out of situations not to stay in them.

FOCUS

When your focus is right, your decisions become right. The greatest amendments of life are not written by partakers of them, but by those who lived them. The real story is better told by the owner of it.

The reason why most of us have no direction in life is because we can't focus. Some of these life choices are not planned, we fall into them because we want to achieve quickly. We have no plan but we want to achieve it. The mind is a very powerful weapon; with misdirection, it can choose even wrong directions when it faces them.

We should learn to be stable and have concentration in what we do, or else we can even get involved even where it seems to be dry. We need something that will make us see life in a different way. Something that can move us and motivate us to be something.

The elevation of my own consideration does not limit me to resist stability. Most of us move from place to place because we don't have a proper direction or focus, and because we don't believe in ourselves. We need to be settled to be able to know where we are headed; we cannot focus if we don't know where our path is leading. We must have that positive thinking in us for changes to happen.

A collide in misdirection can make us confused. We must have a steady mind and make sure that we are sure of what we want. It's like saying?clear your path before you start anything. Time does not reveal to fix mistakes but be prepared to deal with them.

When we allow negative thoughts, we even tolerate failure. The worst thing that can happen is what we think might happen. The problem is the negative thoughts that we think within us, instead of creating the positive us. We attract negative thoughts within us because of the way we think.

The moment your mind is set on what might happen, who would do this, what will I do, when can I do this is the same moment we change everything about our lives. Life is about taking chances; you will never know the outcomes unless you try. The perfect determinations of change in life are the ones that we make. Our minds can be complex which makes us be able to make choices.

The stage of life is the beginning of success, you go through different processes to reach a destination. You don't just wake up and start achieving; you have to plan first and set goals.

LUG ON

There is a thin line between creating a step and emphasizing it. The best way to modify a challenge is to act as the challenge and be the overcomer of the challenge.

We are misled by challenges to panic because we have not set our minds to be overcomers or to be ready for anything. When you go through a situation what do you do?

Ask for help from someone else because you can't handle the situation yourself but imagine if you set your mind to handle anything at any time. Many people would have less decisive ways of doing something and asking for help but accomplishing it themselves.

Let me give you an example of pain. When you are in pain or depression do you share it with someone else or you face it alone? We make small issues seem to be bigger issues because of what we believe in.

The monotony to love is neither persuaded by feelings nor it's persuaded by whom you love. You can love someone and choose not to love them. It depends on whom you love.

When you love someone and you find out he's not what you thought they were, the feelings are stopped because of whom you loved or not love itself. There's something other than what you think there is. A hinder beyond what is unseen to be seen clearly. Open your eyes and see the world on top of your hands.

UNCHAINED

This is yet another chapter of my life; I have felt a leap year had passed and it feels like I'm living in the past. Of course, change is not really that easy but who am I to really compare what I'm about to face, with what I long faced. I'm not really undermining any obstacle. I hoped that by now there has been a change that makes me hope when I'm feeling hopeless. I even choke in my own thoughts when I think about how I can really try and make it out of what I'm suffocating on.

I know a lot of people struggle with change, they dream to change, and they still hope to change though they fantasize it from what they see. Change is not really something that you walk into. You become it in order to feel it and be it. I have had moments where I felt change was a chore. To every song I came across, change began to be reprise that sounded like it didn't have a meaning to it.

I'm not really sure if I really understand. If I'm still living in the past, or I'm walking through the past. Every time I remember change but it's not easy and it's not too hard either. Sometimes we need to take risks. Just jump and take risks.

This is exactly how I used to feel before I was not changed, empty and my life felt meaningless without God. There is a particular presence that can change everything about you and change your whole life. Ever since I started going to church, I felt like my things were becoming worse, because there is no way you can want to do right, and the devil just sits there and watch you grow out of it. Your good is a threat and it will threaten even the physical.

Either you do right or wrong, you will always be fought. Not everyone will like you, they are those who will pretend and those who will hate you to push you to work hard. I call them enemy helpers, some successful people have made it through because of them.

They have become a blessing to so many people because of their differences and dangerous actions, but don't rejoice to be having enemy helpers. Some when they come into your life, they come to finish you, and some come as your biggest motivation to push you to another level.

REASON FOR YOUR SEASON

Words are not enough to express such burdens I have felt that I carried, or too deep to express how I feel right now. Feels like I'm walking with open wounds in winter. I found myself sincerely, having conversations with myself about the losses and wrong choices that I made. I have found my joy in ways that made me suffocate to breathe and suffocate me from my own dreams. I had eyes yet I had been blind.

You must have a reason for your season. Seasons come and go. But when you show you should know that you must reap soon. Many people want to reap without having had shown anything. A seed germinates when it has been planted. Your success comes to work when you plan hard work and put in work for it. We have minds that tell us that our greatest movement is silence and dreaming. People have had dreams the whole year and they still have them.

Sometimes you have to take risks, you have to make radical prayers and to make sure that you know how you could have done it. Experience gives us the best lesson.

Your season is a change, not a thought when you encounter a season you must change the way you thought to be in the new season. Because you have encountered a different platform in a different way and for a different reason for you to change.

There must be a reason for you to have your season. Your time might come and it finds you not ready or not prepared. Sometimes we have to focus for us to receive our seasons.

TIME OF ASSOCIATION

Time defines who we are and what we can do. It's a source of manipulation that doesn't return but gives us a limitation that we can do little or still achieve in the far end. Time builds us, it also makes us focused and it leads us. Without time we wouldn't have schedules and our way of doing things. Time helps us prepare and know what and when we will do things. Same as time can help us to know what we are about to do at what time, so does our minds.

Your preparation comes from your mind, not time. When you prepare, you create time to have room for understanding and be well organized.

Have you ever thought about what difference you'd have made every thirty minutes of your time if you focused a bit more on working on your goals and planning for your future? Our mind has the power to transform us and make us believe we are nothing at the same time even though we are something.

Time is defined by who we are and what we have done. The pleasures of life are winds that blow from all directions but remember not all winds come in a stable way. We have to learn to choose what to tolerate and not what to tolerate in life, the sun does not come up every day when seasons change.

The same applies to us, tolerating something or someone does not mean you have to spend time with them. This is where we tend to lose the time that we should have used to plan and set our goals. The excess of delivery is the access of wisdom. We need to learn before we can start something. Many of us want to succeed but don't want to learn. There's no knowledge without wisdom and there's no wisdom without knowledge.

The premium of knowing something gives you the key to evaluate and have its conclusion. You can't wake up in the morning and say you are heading to work you have to prepare first. The same applies to succeeding; you plan and prepare before you can try something out.

Our mindsets can create wrong timing and wrong preparations at the wrong time. Everything that is not set at the right time can become wrong. The accusation of everything is not in how we think, but how we see ourselves. There is something that creates timing for everything when you are prepared and that's planning. When your planning is right, your timing becomes right.

Your timing can be another person's wrong time. So, learn to know when specifically your time is. We have people who want to be there at the right time for others, just to hijack when it's not their time. When your time is not now, then plan for it and wait for it.

Your timing association is determined by your seasons and whom you walk with matters the most. There are seasons that end for everyone and you should discern when your time is up with your association. Some people come just to take you two steps, and some come to lift you up. Not everyone you associate with in your destiny means there are there to stay.

A bus can start with you in a distance and no one will know if you will reach there without any faults. Some things are unpredictable, but they can be predicted by looking at the conditions that you see. You have to check all phrases and phases before you acknowledge and certify that you can make it.

Your association can link you to your destiny or link you to your betrayers and your enemies. Sometimes we have to take blind risks and trust people even if we know that they will betray us just so we prove ourselves right. Your timing association is very important, be careful and understand it very well.

There is a time to associate and there is a time to be in a solitary place; God hears you but you also need to hear God. Your association can blind you. We can be so blinded by our love-associate, that when they disappoint us, our capabilities change. Pain on its own can change a focused person in us to become people who don't reckon.

People who destroy our lives and betray us are those who are close to us. It's normal, everyone goes through a chapter in life and certainly, the devil will not send someone else to come and destroy you who doesn't know you.

CHANGE

Your change is a multitude of people. Imagine how many people you could save if you changed and shared your testimony. I normally hear people say they want to change, or someone should change their character or change their ways of thinking. Change is a process, it's a path that takes time and needs a lot of dedication to overcome. It's not easy to change and to change our lives we need to change our thoughts and how we do things.

Change doesn't come to please people. It comes as a way of changing the way we do things and how we have been thinking. For some of us, our change should come in changing a few ways of how we do things or how our schedule has been. When you change, you are putting yourself into a new life that you have never lived; you are personally taking a risk with your life into something that you didn't experience before.

Change can be motivated by some means of character, poverty, and other things. When you change it means something good has to come out of it. Our weaknesses are supposed to motivate us to change not to give up. When you become motivated by your weaknesses, it means you believe you can do better and that you can be better.

Our weaknesses should not be a reason for us to give up. But it should be a reason for us to work hard and be better. When you are focus towards changing, it helps you to overcome obstacles. Obstacles can down our spirits and make us weak or ignorant; they can make us think we are failures.

I had to believe and accept that I am not like other people, entirely not forgetting the fact that we are all different. I am just unique in my own ways and not only through pen and paper but because I have been made to be me and to make a difference. I wake up every day as a changed person from the person I was as of yesterday. I fight with the inner me to be better. My strength can be a motivation to someone who is losing hope. Sometimes I tell people when they take a risk, have hope. Without hope, no one can be able to take risks because they make us have hope that possibly there is a probability of overcoming something.

When you have room for failure and for success, you can never be defeated even when you face any of the two. Because you set your heart to know that your failures, don't mean you are a failure.

There is no such thing as the perfect change time if it's your time to change then it will come. Your situations should cause you to change. Change doesn't just come; it comes to perfect where it's broken. Sometimes we resist change by the way we think and how we give up. Your first attempt is not a weakness it's a test so, the more you get tests the more you know how to succeed and what to change. Mistakes are part of life. I'm sure if you could ask around who hasn't made a mistake no one would agree they haven't made a mistake. Mistakes make us learn to know how to be better.

THE ACT OF TALKING

Talking can't just be talking, it doesn't necessarily mean because you have a mouth you can talk anyway and anyhow. The principle of talking with the power of words is set to change something and create something.

You need to have the act of speaking for you to master the art of speaking with a motive. You have not been designed to be a negative speaker but because our minds and thoughts overthink in situations it makes us think negatively and that's why we tend to lose focus on what we should say and how we should master the art of speaking.

Our act of speaking should motivate us to talk in sense. We create paths with our mouth. A trained speech is a set mind; a thoughtful mind is a transformed mind. You practice what you speak, to act what you speak. As a person, you should set targets and not talk about them without any action. You should imagine beyond what you can talk about and not what you can just see.

The principle of a motivational speaker is meant to enhance, comfort, and edify. But the art of talking is set to lead people. You can't be principled and not know the art of mastering a principle. Your way is not your way alone; involve your crowd when you are talking. Some people normally have conversations alone. They try to create and overcome their inner self persons by talking alone. You first have to believe in yourself before you can stand in front of people and try to convince or talk to them.

To talk is an appointment. You appoint yourself with people to motivate them. So, your motive should be in appointment to what will benefit them also.

The reason why many people have achieved and don't deserve their places is because we want to achieve, but not know how to be stable when in success and this is the reason why some people end up failing and giving up. Because they choose to have shorter routes that are misdirecting rather than routes that are directing them to stabilize their way of achieving.

We are born in success to give birth to small company successors and create jobs. Some people tend to spend their money without thinking and acting upon their dreams even wealthy people have lost a lot in life due to their poor decisions. Our mindsets should make us program beyond what we can do and what we see.

KEEP ON HOPING

Hope is a transformation that gives us the will to expect something. Hope is a reason for you to keep on believing in something and hoping for the best outcomes.

People who have hope are people who are expectant. Even when you don't believe but the fact that you have hope, it uplifts your faith. If we all started something out of hope, some people could have not stopped giving up too early.

Having hope maintains you, it gives you the confidence to have a steady expectant heart. Even when it's dry still you will hope. Hope is equal to our transformation. We tend to pick up stones when our hands are filled with diamonds. Our conditions make us not to see beyond what is before us. We lose hope because we never had room to be expectant to win or to fail. When you fail even during storms you should still be expectant. This type of hope, I'm referring to, is having hope even when there is nothing.

What you tolerate is what you accept. Hope gives us assurance that it will happen. It cordially gives us an expected key to keep on believing no matter what happens.

WILL I MAKE IT

Many people have a syndrome of "will I make it?" "Can I do it?" "Should I try it?" "Will it work?" No one ever did anything knowing if they will make it or not. Life is like medicine; your perception of it will yield the same results. In life, you should know what you are doing and how to do it.

People are so concerned about what the future holds for them; life is about taking risks. Walking out of your doorstep every morning and facing the world is a risk. The same as being worried about your future. Take a risk and have hope.

You will never know unless you maintain and take a risk. Life is built on, "I will make it" type of mentality. Believe in yourself that you will make it no matter what.

The reason why you question your mind is because you were never ready to face anything or to start anything. Life doesn't just rise from zero to hero with no equal effort to what you want. Your biggest challenge is not setting your mind to overcome challenges but learning how to overcome them.

You can start something and it works out well, and you can still do the same thing and it works out well. The power behind all of this is, "life is a win or lose" but it doesn't mean stop what you are doing.

Our problem as people is we set paces before us to our success even before God can even intervene. We are always too fast and too eager to move without His voice.

BE SET

A trained mind is a set mind; a focused mind is a transformed mind. You practice what you preach demonstrated by your actions. As a person, you should set targets not and talk about them without any action. You should imagine beyond where you can go and not what you could have done.

We have people who still live in regrets and give up. The act of not trying again means you were not ready. A leader directs and not misleads. People are so anxious about knowing the steps to set up a proper life. How about having the proper set up?

They say rules are meant to be broken, but they are set to lead people therefore they must never be made to be broken. Your set up is your start up. The way you present everything is the way you start everything. How you start matters the most. Wrong foundations come from wrong intentions and wrong intentions come from wrong formations. The way you start determines how you will end and continue.

You have to be set and ready for anything that you do. We are born in success to give birth to small company successors. Your set up is your future start up again.

The way you do things gives you a clear probability of how you will make it in life. You have to plan before you take any decision on how to do things.

There is no start up without a start plan. Your goals are not everyone's goal, your vision is not what other people want to know or see. Get to know your set up before you can be set.

THE CROSS OVER

Dream beyond measures, write beyond measure but don't suffer beyond measures.

We are not weighed by where we come from, or where we have been. We are weighed by situations and how we change them. Your past doesn't direct you; it leads you. We all have choices, and for a minute if we could all take time to think before we act and transform the way we view things a lot of us could have made good decisions.

We are born beyond measures, how we think it's either it directs us or misdirects us. As a person how you measure your standards or your worth is how you will end up. Thinking beyond measures gives you the advantage to go beyond and think beyond where you can go.

I always tell people to imagine it's possible. Meaning the possibility of it and its probability of happening can be possible. With a total transformation into our lives, we are allowed to choose to be who we want to be.

To go beyond measure means you are ready for the challenges that you may face while facing your path. When doing something be ready for anything, but never choose to give up. To fail is to choose to give up, failure doesn't mean give up, but it means try again and again until you achieve something.

A lot of people become depressed when they fail instead of using failure as their strengths. Have you ever considered there might be someone out there who's better at what you do, and you still have a long way to go? Sometimes when you fail to compare your worth and try doing more in what you do. The reason why we allow stress or failure to control us is because we are not ready to face anything or even to achieve what we want to achieve. Your determination to what you do should make you not give up. It should give you the inspiration to keep on pushing and working harder no matter what. You are at the edge of your crossover and only you can determine how you will make it. It is not your own will unless you make it to be your will.

PURPOSE

Create a potential purpose in everything you do. Ask yourself why you are doing; what you are doing; when do you want to do it; who are you doing it for; where do you want to do it and how will you do it.

Generate something that will create a purpose for someone to have a drive in life. Relate and have a proper market for your project. The thing that values purpose the most is effort; learn to put effort in what you want to achieve for it to have a meaning and move on.

There should be a voice in your silence that gives you purpose to create something out of yourself or what you may want to offer.

Some people may feel the urge to buy something because of its quality. In the market, we find that quality and price speak louder to consumers. People incline to the belief that quality and price are equal and the lower the price then the less value or quality.

So, always make sure that such mentality doesn't exist in your purpose where people tend to question if their money is worth a product or a project you are doing. Some products or projects don't need to have a purpose; they should speak for themselves and raise awareness for themselves. The more powerful the product or the project the more people give you free advertising about it.

Purpose should be given in everything and every way where it's most needed. Customers tend to ask themselves questions such as why should I; where should I; is it good enough; I am sure I can put my money on this; would it really work as I think. A good product or project cancels a mind with the wrong mentality and wrong thinking. There's no way you can create chaos where there is no chaos. Great ideas take you to great places, invest and commit to producing quality. People like quality products and quality sells. Because it is said "the first impression is the last impression. You can't expect people to buy poor quality from a new source that has not built a reputation with them. You value your product by what you produced.

Customers value time, income, and products. Without a stable product, they tend to be disappointed and they may end up tarnishing your name.

BE WISE

Every single one of us has a gift and that gift is not defined by what one has or what one can do, but it is defined by what they have done.

A lot of gifted people wait for opportunities to come to them while they should be looking for them. It is written and mentioned that "Seek and it shall be given to you". It's like looking for a job and having qualifications and you wait for a job to come to you. Some possibilities need us to act upon them so that they could work therefore without hard work and there will be no results at the end of the day. You have to learn how to use your gift before you can use it just like at school. You learn and go through a test before you can pass it.

A gift can come in forms and levels. But how you commit to your gift will determine how far you will go. We are not led by what we have, but how far we can go? A gift moves you from one place to another. So, to have full access to it, you should commit to it.

The way you operate in your gift can be different from how others operate. We are not moved by what other people have, but what we have and how we can use it. So, the reason why other people envy others is because they want what they don't have and what is not theirs.

BE MOTIVATED

Your weaknesses are supposed to motivate you to see the better you. If it weren't for them, you wouldn't have known what you are capable to do beyond them. Not all of us who try out things become victors, some of us are destined for greater objectives and we have to go through holes that we can't dig and come out of them to make it in life.

Be patient in life and have perseverance. An objective can be an opinion but does not qualify you to decide. If you are giving up because of failure, you were not ready to succeed. You should be prepared and also know trials are meant to shift and later position you to a place you are meant to be. Having failed, what you intended to achieve does not mean you can never achieve it. It is somehow a form of motivation for improving and doing better than what you could have done. Failure shed some light between right and wrong or even the level at which they fall. Your competitors should motivate you, not intimidate you.

POWER

Power doesn't rate us, but it's given to other people to control us with it. Many people tend to lose their way when they have power, and some get to an extent of mistreating people with it.

Power is not supposed to be a limitation, it's supposed to be a direction and make us understand what we are supposed to do with the people who possess it.

It is a tendency for people to blame those who have power. But the question is what did you do to make sure that the person who possesses the power and misuses it doesn't do that.

We hold the power to acknowledge our strengths in life; we are given authority so that they may be in order. Not everyone gets the privilege to have power. Some people are leaders because they have leadership skills and it's for them to make sure that there is a direction in what is being done and how it will be done. This means, in other words, power is given to make sure that there is a direction and to lead people.

CHALLENGES

Everyone has challenges in life even in business there are so many challenges. Everyone faces challenges; there is no one who doesn't go through challenges. Sometimes we face challenges to discover our strongest moments.

Challenges come in different ways, at times you may face challenges because of the place that you are in. The place that you find yourself in at times can be the reason for what you go through at times.

Challenges are a burden; you carry reasons to start something new or to be something new because of what you have. Your reason to do something or to face something can be because of what you have or what you have done. Your reason for having something can be the reason why you face challenges. When the timing is wrong, nothing is right. Whatever you may be facing can be because of the wrong timing that you chose to accommodate. Some people fall into plans at the wrong time. And some people fall into challenges because of being involved with the crowd at the wrong time.

YOUR TRIAL IS A TESTIMONY

I don't really know if self-love describes us more. Our hearts are bound, and we forget that to give is to get. You cannot receive if you are not prepared to give.

Let me tell you something, what you are going through is passing through winds. There are winds that are there to make us move to the next level. Don't give up yet. You might feel, you are probably the only one who is going through a lot.

Everyone receives challenges and how you face them determines how you will overcome them. Your tests can never be bigger than what you can't handle. Your tests are how big you are.

Don't overweigh yourself. Always position yourself. A positioned mind is a mind that has direction. We all need freedom but when it's inside of us. The moment you earn to create it, you will learn to overcome any small obstacle.

I have encountered situations in life and I wanted to give up on business. I asked myself why all this was happening to me. If not me, then who? I had so many thoughts and challenges I was facing and people who were against me were increasing and this made me stronger.

There were times I asked myself if I was my own mentor, what advice would I have given myself and would I have had given up? How would people who believe in me take it in if I was to give up now? It is not about people but about me and my vision or where I want to be. Why give up now when I went through all this. Being an entrepreneur is not easy. You go through persecutions and you lose a lot to gain.

An entrepreneur is likely to be backstabbed in the business, but an ambitious and visionary entrepreneur becomes strong to overcome every challenge and obstacle. I was depressed, hurt and drained. I spent my days in bed and regretting, but I asked myself why I started in the first place. Hope won't help me, but using my weaknesses to get up will help me.

It was church, business and family. One season package, as a whole, was drowning me. I couldn't balance and I couldn't cope with all the stress I was going through. I would sometimes go outside and feel better and not know how I got there. I was deeply slopping in and dying yet I'm alive.

I remember telling my mother about my problems and she told me to come back home, I needed to hear get up and work but she made me more comfortable and I felt I needed a few harsh words to make me strong. God kept telling me to wake up, even when I was walking, I would hear Him saying "wake up and rise up."

I was committed at church 24/7 and I was wondering why I'm going through all of this. I kept losing customer after customer and you can wonder how many customers wanted a refund from me because I had lost business. I lost money, I lost myself and I lost my direction of which came to me in understanding that God can break you just to position you. Here is the thing, God being silent in the midst of your problems doesn't mean there is no sign.

Sometimes you go through things to be able to help people who go through things also. You go through a lot so that God can be able to position you. Your trails can come just so that they position you. Your tests are your breakthrough. I couldn't handle the stress and pain and I felt like giving up was the only option. Sometimes you ask for help from people and when they are not of help, you tend to hate them or you feel no one cares, sometimes you need God. People can't help you or mend you, but God can. It takes prayer to change situations don't give up your story is about to change.

I was homeless, broken spiritually, broke, lost, depressed and in debts. I remember listening to people testifying about how God has taken them from situations. How God has helped them in so many ways. So those testimonies helped me have more faith.

It takes prayer to change situations and your end can be your beginning. A delay doesn't mean silence and denial. Your story is about to change. I remember all my friends betraying me and backstabbing me. The devil will not go as far as a stranger to mess with your destiny, it's the ones who are close to us that destroy us. It becomes painful to be betrayed by those who are next to you and it makes you lose hope also. I was very hurt and so disappointed in a way that I lost a lot of people in my life.

We are broken to be mended. I'm not sure what you might be going through, but let me tell you this, you are coming out of that situation.

I remember Prophetic Pastor Phitshane preaching and he said, "you don't have to struggle", from there I knew I was coming out of all of my situations. If he said it, I know it's possible. In every season there is a test and there is a breakthrough that you should receive. The higher the anointing the bigger the opposition and the bigger the position the bigger the oppositions will come.

I went to Pretoria on the 8th, 2018 for a stewardship summit at Enlightened Christian Church. My heart was not really on the event but on the purpose of my breakthrough as I was looking for freedom from all of this. On a Saturday when we were supposed to come back, I just couldn't go back the same. Something in me told me to still hold on and keep on hoping. I had to make sure I attend the Sunday service.

My story had to change no matter what. When I got there, I listened to the testimonies which were being said, as the other man testified about how he was locked outside the house and he lost his job and after Major 1 located him his life changed, the other one talked about how he used his last money to go to Pretoria and ever since then his life changed. But then there was a lady who had cancer which was spreading to her brain and she got healed.

There is no situation that God cannot mend or solve. Your trials come to position you. I stood up and knew if cancer can be healed so can my situations change. I mean I was crying for a financial breakthrough and someone had cancer.

When Major 1 started preaching it blew me away it's as if he was talking about me. He said, "God will allow you to suffer first for sometimes before perfecting you. Sometimes it's better to understand the calling than the problem. God will allow you to go through problems in order for Him to perfect you."

I came out there changed, I'm not sure how I got out the door, but the message blew me away. I was shocked and from that moment no matter what I went through, I was willing to face all of it. There is no destiny that comes without a process. The process breaks us and changes us.

Sometimes we drown in depression and pain because we are willing to live in joy but not willing to handle what joy might bring. I was homeless, broken spiritually, depressed and in debts but all I learnt to know God and seek God in all situations I go through. God breaks us to mend us.

My heart was always in pain thinking that I'm always in pain and I serve God but why me. The question is, if not me then who should it be? I met people and some people turned against me. I felt caged and uncaged. I couldn't leave well.

Every day it became worse. I prayed and I fasted and the more I fasted it felt like I was making things worse. That's the thing when near your breakthrough the devil will make sure he takes out your focus.

Your best focus doesn't come from focusing on your problems but knowing how big is your God.

I met friends who changed my life. I came to understand God in a very close perspective. When you put your trust in worries you will get worries. I remember my friend telling me to have faith in God, as faith is bigger than hope and as it does not fail even though hope is what most of us believe in. Sometimes when everything fell apart, I didn't understand. We kept praying and it didn't make sense at all.

Sometimes it doesn't have to make sense, child of God. God is the one who is in control, not you. God has it all planned out for you. I lost friends to receive a friend, I could learn a lot from them. I found my inner peace with God and in God. I came to realize that our position needs to be broken so God guides us and directs us to the right people in life.

Without inner peace, you will shake even when problems come. My words for you is to "keep holding on no matter which storm comes and they won't make you fall."